JEAN DE BRUNHOFF

Babar's Friend Zephir

A Magnet Book

Other Babar stories in Magnet Books

Babar's Travels
Babar the King
Babar at Home
Babar and Father Christmas

First published in Great Britain 1937
by Methuen & Co Ltd
This edition first published 1965
This Magnet edition first published 1987
by Methuen Children's Books Ltd
11 New Fetter Lane, London EC4P 4EE
Copyright © Librairie Hachette, Paris
Printed in Great Britain
by Scotprint Ltd, Musselburgh

ISBN 0 416 08962 3

In Celesteville the school of the elephants had broken up for the summer.

The little monkey Zephir, like all his schoolfellows, left for the holidays. How delightful to see his family again! But how sad to part from his friends, King Babar, Queen Celeste, his schoolmistress, the Old Lady, and his dear Arthur! All four had promised him to come down to the river near the bridge, to wish him for the last time a happy journey.

There they were! Zephir saw them. He waved his handkerchief, and cried: "Good-bye!"

Zephir arrived at the station in the Town of the Monkeys, and threw himself into his mother's arms.

"How you have grown, my dear!" she said,
as she embraced him.

Zephir and all his family squeezed into their car. Zephir sat in front with his father; his mother sat behind with his little sister and his brothers.

"All aboard!" cried Zephir. "Drive as fast as you can!"

There was a rope ladder to climb, to reach their house at the top of a tree.

Zephir ran up easily; but he laughed as he thought to himself, "This is no way for elephants!"

The house in which Zephir's family lived was not large, but it was comfortable. While his mother prepared an excellent soup of bananas in chocolate, Zephir played at hide-and-seek with his brothers. His father carried up the suitcases, and his little sister sat on the swing.

Zephir went to bed, and fell asleep at once. But in the middle of the night he was awakened by the nightingale, singing very loudly: "Troulala, Tiou-tiou-tiou! Tidi! Tidi!"

He jumped quickly out of bed and ran to the window, crying, "Welcome, my dear old friend!"

How Zephir and his old friend the nightingale gossiped!
    "Do you know," said the nightingale breathlessly,
"that there is a large package, addressed to you, waiting
at the station? And under the address is written, 'From
Babar'."
    "Perhaps it is a piano," Zephir replied. "I won the first
prize for music."

The next morning Zephir ran to the station.
What a wonderful surprise! Babar had sent him a real boat.
With the help of his father, he pushed it towards the sea.

He bathed and fished, as the elephants had taught him to do.
The monkeys admired him, for they were frightened of the water,
and the Princess Isabel said to her father, General Huc:
"Oh, how brave Zephir is!"

"Whatever have I caught?" Zephir cried in amazement, when he saw the mermaid in his net.

And then the beautiful creature began to speak: "Oh! Mr. Monkey," she said, "don't hold me so tight. You are hurting me. Do listen to what I have to say. I am a very little mermaid and I live in the sea. I have a head and arms, like you, but I have a fish's tail. I am used to a life in the sea. If you take me to your forests I shall die.

"Let me go back to swim with my sisters. My name is Eleanor. Perhaps one day you will need my help. If you do, throw three pebbles into the sea, and call my name three times. Wherever I may be, I shall hear you and come. I shall never forget you."

Zephir listened to the little mermaid and carefully unhooked her. He let her go, but he was rather sad at having lost her.

On his way home, after his fishing adventure, Zephir saw
many of the monkeys reading newspapers, and he heard the
news-monkeys shouting, "Special Edition! Disappearance of
the Princess Isabel!"

"Poor little girl!" he thought. "I can't believe it! She was
standing on the shore this morning when I went fishing."

He listened to the talk going on around him, and this is
what he heard: Isabel was playing in the palace gardens when
suddenly a green cloud enveloped her and hid her from her
friends. It lifted her into the air, leaving behind it a strong smell
of rotten apples. Since then the Princess had not been seen.

General Huc, overcome with grief and anxiety, mustered his guard, and gave his orders to Colonel Aristobald.

"General," this brave officer replied, "I promise you that we will leave no stone unturned to find the Princess, your daughter."

In the air, on the water, in the trees, on the mountains, and through the brushwood, Aristobald and his soldiers searched for the Princess. But in spite of all their efforts, they found no trace of her.

General Huc arrived in his car to hear the latest news. In answer to his questions, the Colonel hung his head sadly. The General understood, and went away with a heavy heart.

Only Zephir still had hopes of finding the Princess. Secretly, he put in his knapsack a bottle of water and some provisions. He also took his most treasured possessions – his violin and his clown's costume. Then he set out towards the sea.

Happily the shore was deserted. He picked up three pebbles and threw them into the water, crying three times: "Eleanor, my dear friend, Zephir is here, waiting for you!"

Just as she had promised, the little mermaid appeared.

"Isabel is lost," he told her. "Can you help me to find her?"

"It will be difficult," she replied, "but for your sake I will do my best. Wait for me, and I will fetch my carriage."

A few minutes later, seated in a giant cockle-shell, Zephir felt happy, because they were on the move. The racing fish pulled well.

Eleanor guided them to a wild-looking island, and, pointing to it, said: "My Aunt Crustadel lives there. We will go to her grotto to see her. She will give us good advice."

"My children," said Crustadel, after having listened to them in silence, "he who smells like a rotten apple, he who has taken away Isabel, is Polomoche."

"Who is Polomoche?" Zephir asked.

"He is a monster who lives on his island with his friends the Gogottes. They live on grass and fruit, and are not fierce, but they are bored. From time to time, for a change, Polomoche goes on a voyage seated in a little green cloud. If he meets an animal that attracts him, he carries it home. That is what has happened to Isabel.

"He is capricious and impatient, and he has a bad habit of changing those who anger him into stones.

"Little monkey, if you wish to save your Princess you have not a moment to lose. Eleanor will go with you, and wait for you. Take this old sack: it will be useful to you. And remember, you must make Polomoche laugh if you wish to succeed. You will recognise him by his pointed horns and his yellow skin.

"Go quickly, and be brave!"

After a good crossing, Eleanor and Zephir disembarked
without having been seen by the Gogottes.

    The landscape was gloomy. They would have liked
to run away; they did not speak. Zephir held his little
friend's hand in his.

Over his clothes and his light luggage Zephir drew on
the sack given him by Crustadel. When he had done so,
he looked like one of the stones with which the island
was covered.

   He climbed slowly up towards the top of the hill,
thinking deeply of his plan.

When he arrived at the top he heard a gruff voice. Quickly he took off his sack and peeped out between the boulders. Isabel was there, in the midst of the monsters!

"Lady Monkey," Polomoche was grumbling, "I kidnapped you because I thought you amusing, and now you do nothing but cry! I have had enough of it. I shall change you into a stone."

"My Lord Polomoche, and you, Ladies and Gentlemen Gogottes, I salute you," Zephir said politely, as he suddenly disclosed himself. "I am a clown-musician by profession. Allow me to stay here and I will amuse you."

Isabel recognised him, and letting fall her handkerchief, thought: "Ah, it is high time he came!"

Soon, thanks to Zephir, everyone was happy.
A quiet gaiety reigned. He told them stories:
about the rat who had an elephant's trunk, about
the blind huntsman, about the macaroni cannon
and the Captain Hoplala, about Thorough-wax
and Filigree.

And every time that he came to the end of one,
Polomoche and the Gogottes begged him for
another: "Another! Tell us another!"

When he was tired of telling stories, Zephir put on his clown's costume. How lucky that he had brought it with him!

"Cuckoo!" he cried. "I will now show the game of hunting the magic cat."

Having spoken these words, he did every trick he could think of to make his audience laugh.

He dropped his hat – and thump! he fell as he dived after it. Then, springing up, he turned a somersault. When at last he caught his hat with his tail, Polomoche roared with laughter.

"Now!" thought the cunning Zephir, "one more little
effort and the time will be ripe. My plan is a good one.
Tomorrow we will be far away."

    Picking up his violin, he played polkas and waltzes
without a stop. Polomoche and the Gogottes, carried
away by the music, jumped about, turning and
pirouetting.

So tired were they at last, that they lay down
in a heap, snoring peacefully. Zephir quickly changed,
and prepared for flight.
     "Now is the moment," he whispered to Isabel,
and they ran as fast as they could towards the sea.
     From a distance Eleanor waved to them.

They were saved! Land was in sight! Polomoche and the Gogottes still slept.

On their way, Zephir and his companions thanked Crustadel. Some birds had signalled their arrival, and the news spread quickly.

From all sides the monkeys came running. Some ran to the beach; others looked on from the cliffs. General Huc brought out his telescope. Zephir's family cried for joy.

Our two heroes were garlanded with flowers by the enthusiastic crowd. They had said goodbye to the gentle Eleanor, who had returned to her home, drawn by her fishes.

Before the soldiers of his guard, the General complimented Zephir, and said: "My young friend, I, General Huc, President of the Republic of the Monkeys, am proud of you, and I give you the hand of my beloved daughter Isabel. You shall marry her when you are old enough."

When Zephir returned to his home after the ceremony, his father and his mother, his sister and his brothers, made a great fuss of him.

They were so pleased to see him again, that they never scolded him for having gone away without warning them and for having caused them so much anxiety.

They danced with him and sang: "Long live the newly betrothed!"

After beginning with this exciting adventure,
the holidays finished quietly and happily.

Zephir returned to Celesteville. As long as he
remains with the elephants, Eleanor and her
sisters will keep watch over Isabel.